RAZZLE DAZZLE
goes to town

written by
Joseph Gray

illustrated by
Mariella Travis

For
Cori, Katie, Owen
and Little Miss Isla.
Dedicated to Mothers
around the world.

Little Razzle Dazzle

woke up, as usual, with a smile on his little round face.

Today was extra **special!**

Razzle was headed to town for a special gift.

He hopped out of bed and made his usual breakfast of toast and homemade

Razzle Dazzle Berry Jam.

Razzle looked out the window upon his little secret garden and said hello to all of his friends.

"Razzle Dazzle Do!"

That is how Razzle said hello to his good friends and family.

"Hello Wazzle"
McBirdy the chickadee tweeted.

"Hello, hello"
McBirdy had a hard time with his R's.

"Good morning Sammy"
Razzle shouted to Mr. Samuel Chipmunk.

"Good Morning Everyone!"

Razzle shouted with a big smile.

It was time to get dressed. Being a special day, Razzle Dazzle had to put on a special walking-to-town outfit. Comfy shorts, t-shirt and his hiking shoes. He was wearing his favorite shirt with a big tall giraffe on it. Razzle hoped one day, to be as tall as Gerald the Giraffe, who lived at the **Bizzly Dizzly Zoo.**

Razzle always giggled when he called Gerald "Gerry" in front of his friends. Gerry was well-known for showing up in unusual locations. One time, he was found **standing on his head** in front of the monkey house.

Finally Razzle Dazzle headed into town, about a 5 minute walk, on a **razzleberry colored brick road.**

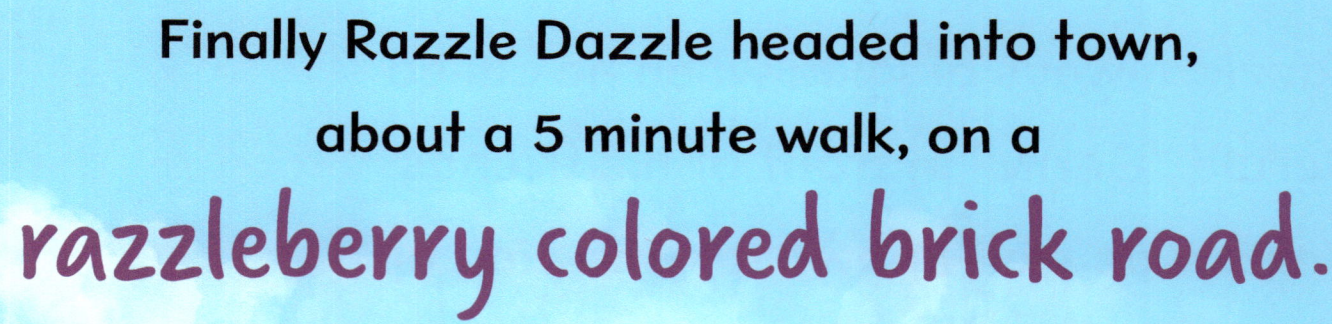

As he entered town, all of the merchants shouted happy greetings to Razzle. They loved to see his smiling friendly face. Razzle never complained about prices and always had kind words for the shop owners.

Razzle hoped to own his own Chocolate Drizzle Shop one day, and tried very hard to treat people the way he would like to be treated.

"Morning Razzly" said the butcher. "I've some fine pork chops on special today!"

"No thank you" replied little Razzly Dazzly Do "I am all set today. I bet your pork chops are delicious!"

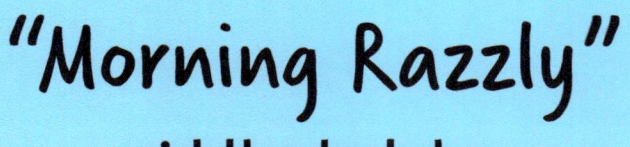

"Mmmm" Razzle smelled yummy cookies.

"Hi Dazzler" shouted Mrs. Bakerooni "I have some yummy cookies for you."

"No, thank you" replied Razzle "I bet they are delicious, but not today."

On Razzle went, past the honey shop where Mr. Bizz Bazz Buzz was hard at work.

"How about some yummy honey, Razz?"

"Not today. You have the best honey around. I have it on my RazzleDazzleBerry toast! I will see you soon Mr. Bizzy."

Razzle continued on his way,
singing his favorite song.

"A razzly dazzly do
and a razzly dazzly doh,
a razzly dazzly dizzly do!"

At last, Razzle had reached his favorite shop!

The little Flowery Wowzy Petalicious Shop.

He knew just what he wanted.

A big bouquet of **daffodillzys** and **mumzy wumzys**.

This made Dazzly so happy!

Wahoozler!

Razzle ran all the way home,

past the shops,

down the river,

up the razzleberry brick path.

"Mom...MOM...MOMMA!!"

He shouted

"Razzly Dazzly Do!"

He gave his mom a big hug.

She was his *favorite* person in the whole world.

His big trip to town was a huge success!

Copyright © 2024 Joseph Gray
www.josephgraysculpture.com

First Edition — 2024

Illustration, cover design and formatting by Mariella Travis | www.alleiram.com

All rights reserved.

No part of this publication may be reproduced in any form, or by any means, electronic or mechanical, including photocopying, recording, or any information browsing, storage, or retrieval system, without permission in writing from the author and illustrator.

ISBN:
979-8-218-52916-1 (Paperback)
979-8-218-52940-6 (Hardcover)

IMPRINT: JOSEPH GRAY (INDEPENDENTLY PUBLISHED)

Milton Keynes UK
Ingram Content Group UK Ltd.
UKHW052214011124
450591UK00003B/42